CARROT
THE GOLDFISH

by

SOPHIE HANNAH

Illustrated by Jean Baylis

HAMISH HAMILTON
LONDON

To Dan with love

HAMISH HAMILTON LTD

Published by the Penguin Group
27 Wrights Lane, London w8 5tz, England
Penguin Books USA Inc., 375 Hudson Street, New York, New York 10014, USA
Penguin Books Australia Ltd, Ringwood, Victoria, Australia
Penguin Books Canada Ltd, 10 Alcorn Avenue, Toronto, Ontario, Canada m4v 3b2
Penguin Books (NZ) Ltd, 182–190 Wairau Road, Auckland 10, New Zealand

Penguin Books Ltd, Registered Offices: Harmondsworth, Middlesex, England

First published in Great Britain 1992 by Hamish Hamilton Ltd

1 3 5 7 9 10 8 6 4 2

British Library Cataloguing in Publication Data
CIP data for this book is available from the British Library

ISBN 0-241-13211-8

Set in 15pt Baskerville by Rowland Phototypesetting Ltd
Bury St Edmunds, Suffolk
Printed in Great Britain by BPCC Hazells Ltd
Member of BPCC Ltd

Chapter One

Bobby was so hungry that his stomach was rumbling. He went into the kitchen where Mum was busy cooking.

"What's for lunch?" he asked.

"Vegetable stew," said Mum.

There were vegetables all over the kitchen: potatoes, turnips, cauliflower, onions and carrots. Looking at them made Bobby

feel even hungrier.

"I'm starving," he moaned. "When will lunch be ready?"

Mum frowned at him crossly. "If you're so impatient, why don't you come and help me prepare it?" she suggested.

"I can't cook," Bobby protested. Mum laughed. "You don't have to cook, silly! You could just help me by peeling the carrots."

Bobby sighed. Why had he opened his big mouth?

"Come on," said Mum, firmly. "Here's the peeler."

Bobby began to peel the carrots, making the kitchen even messier than it already was. Bits of carrot peel flew everywhere.

"Do you have to make such a mess?" Mum asked.

But Bobby wasn't listening to her. His mind was on something completely different. Tomorrow was April Fool's Day, and Bobby still hadn't managed to think of a good trick to play on his grandma.

He and Grandma always played tricks on each other on April Fool's Day, and it was a competition to see who could play the better and cleverer trick. Grandma usually won, but Bobby consoled himself with the thought that Grandma was a lot older than he was. She was seventy-five, so she'd had a lot more practice than Bobby had at April Fools.

But Bobby was still determined to

win this year. If only he could just think of a brilliant trick. Suddenly Mum's voice brought Bobby out of his daydream.

"Bobby, please try not to get carrot peel absolutely everywhere! Look, you've even flicked a bit into my glass of water."

Bobby looked. True enough, there was a large sliver of carrot peel floating in Mum's glass. Bobby began to laugh.

"What's so funny?" asked Mum.

"It looks like a goldfish!" Bobby giggled. "That piece of carrot peel looks exactly like a goldfish!"

"Mm, I suppose it does," said Mum, chopping up an onion. "Have you nearly finished those carrots?"

Bobby did not answer her. He had just had a wonderful idea, one of the best he'd ever had. This was the perfect April Fool! Grandma's eyesight was very bad. She might believe that this piece of carrot peel was actually a goldfish. Bobby couldn't wait to find out!

"Mum," he said. "I can't help you any more. I've got to do something else. It's very important."

"Oh, really?" Mum smiled. "Am I allowed to know what it is?"

"Not yet," said Bobby. "It's a brilliant idea I've had for an April Fool trick to play on Grandma. I think I might win this year."

"It must be very good," said Mum, doubtfully. "Grandma's tricks are pretty hard to beat!"

Bobby hid a bit of carrot peel in
his pocket and ran upstairs to his
bedroom. There was a glass bowl full
of flowers on his shelf. He took the
flowers out, filled the bowl up with
water and dropped the carrot peel in.

9

Delighted, Bobby stood back and admired his work. Now the piece of carrot peel looked even more like a goldfish because it was in a proper goldfish bowl. Carrot the Goldfish, Bobby thought happily to himself.

He could hardly wait until tomorrow. He set his alarm clock to wake him up at seven o'clock. You had to play April Fool tricks before midday, or they didn't count. And then if Grandma fell for the trick, as Bobby was sure she would, he could tell her the truth at twelve o'clock. Bobby imagined how much she would laugh. Grandma loved a good trick!

Meanwhile, in her house a little further down the road, Grandma was also thinking about April Fool's Day. It was a special occasion for her and Bobby, almost as much fun as birthdays and Christmas. Grandma was an expert practical joke player. She was proud of this talent, and she knew that Bobby got as much pleasure from her tricks as she did from his. That was why she was so worried. Usually she started preparing her trick long before April Fool's Day, but this time she had been so busy that she still hadn't thought of one. Grandma knew how disappointed Bobby would be if she didn't play an April Fool on him this year, so she racked her brains to try and think of one. But nothing came to mind.

"Oh well," Grandma thought to herself. "I've got all day to think of one."

But then she suddenly remembered that she had to go and collect her new glasses.

14

"At least I'll be able to see properly then," Grandma said to herself. "And it's much easier to think properly when you can see properly."

She was determined to think of the perfect trick, and win the competition again this year!

Chapter Two

The next morning was April Fool's
Day. Bobby's alarm went off at seven
o'clock sharp. Usually he liked to lie
in for a few minutes and doze, but
this morning he was so excited that
he jumped out of bed immediately
and got dressed as quickly as he
could. His heart was beating faster
than ever, and he had that funny,
wobbly feeling in his stomach which

16

he always got when he was nervous.
Mum and Dad were still asleep, and
Bobby tiptoed downstairs so as not
to wake them. He held the glass bowl
with its piece of carrot peel carefully.

In the hall, he wrote a note on a scrap of paper saying: 'Gone to Grandma's. Back soon.' Then he closed the front door as quietly as he could and set off. Grandma's house was only a minute's walk away. She and Bobby lived on the same road.

Looking at his watch, Bobby realised that it was only quarter past seven. What if Grandma wasn't awake yet? But she would be. Even though she was older, Grandma got just as excited as Bobby did at the prospect of April Fool's Day.

Grandma's house was a bungalow and it was painted a nice, warm rosy colour. Bobby loved going there because it reminded him of a country cottage, even though it was right in the middle of a big town.

Grandma was sitting in her big, brown armchair in front of the window as Bobby walked up the garden path. She waved at him and smiled cheerfully, getting up to answer the door. Grandma felt very guilty. She simply hadn't been able to think of a trick. She would have to admit this to Bobby and hope that he didn't mind too much.

But before she had a chance to say a word, Bobby began to speak quickly and excitedly.

"Hello, Grandma," he said.
"Look! I've got a present for you."

He handed her the bowl with the
carrot peel in it.

"It's a pet goldfish. Do you like
it?"

Bobby's heart thumped wildly.
Would she fall for his trick or not?

Grandma looked at her present.
She could see a lot better with her

new glasses. This was a very strange
goldfish indeed, she thought. It
wasn't moving at all and it didn't
seem to have a face. Suddenly,
Grandma realised that this present
was Bobby's April Fool trick. It
wasn't a goldfish at all, it was a piece
of carrot peel! She was about to say,

"What a clever trick!" when she had a better idea. She would pretend to be fooled and play an even craftier trick on Bobby. She knew exactly what to do.

"Thank you!" she said. "It's lovely. I've always wanted a goldfish!"

She gave Bobby a big hug.

Grandma was a round, cuddly sort of old lady, not a skinny, bony one. Bobby's other grandmother was skinny and bony, and not half as nice to hug as his round, cuddly Grandma.

"What a lovely present!" Grandma exclaimed. "What shall I call him?"

Bobby grinned nervously. "How about Carrot?" he suggested.

"Carrot!" Grandma beamed happily. "That's the perfect name for him! He even looks a bit like a carrot!"

Bobby was thrilled that Grandma had fallen for his trick. He wondered whether he should tell her the truth now, so that they could both have a good laugh about it. But Grandma was already talking to Carrot the Goldfish.

"Come and sit on the table over here," she was saying cheerfully. "What a pretty goldfish you are! Oh, how lucky I am to have you!"

Bobby began to feel a bit guilty. He hadn't expected Grandma to get so attached to Carrot so quickly. Would she be very disappointed? He had never meant to upset her.

"Bobby, I've got lots of things to do this morning," said Grandma. "Why don't you go home now and come back again at about eleven? Besides, I've got to go out and buy some special goldfish food for Carrot. Oh, it's so exciting!"

Bobby walked home slowly, wondering what to do. Grandma had seemed so pleased about the goldfish.

What a mess he'd got himself into! He'd have to tell Grandma eventually, and what would she say?

Maybe I'll buy her a real goldfish out of my pocket money, Bobby thought, so that she won't be too upset. He decided to go and ask Mum about it.

Grandma put on her hat and coat and went to the pet shop in town.

"I'd like to buy a goldfish," she said to the man behind the counter. There were lots of goldfish in the

shop: big ones, small ones, fat ones and thin ones. Eventually Grandma bought a small thin one because it was a similar shape to the piece of carrot peel that Bobby had given her.

"Now I've got a real goldfish!" she said to herself happily. "And I'm going to play the best trick on Bobby that I've ever played."

Grandma called her new goldfish Carrot. After all, it was a very good name for a goldfish. She took Carrot home and put him in the bowl that Bobby had given her. She fished the bit of carrot peel out of the water and threw it away. Laughing, she sat down and waited for Bobby to come back.

Chapter Three

Bobby told Mum about his brilliant
April Fool and how it had gone
wrong. Mum laughed.

"Don't worry," she said.
"Grandma can take a joke. And you
can buy her a real goldfish if you
want to. That would be nice. But you
should go round now and tell her the
truth."

Bobby looked at his watch. It was

nearly eleven. Surely Grandma would be back now? He felt slightly better after talking to Mum about it. If Mum thought it would be all right then it probably would. And besides, Grandma had only had Carrot the Goldfish for a few hours. She couldn't possibly be that attached to it, Bobby reassured himself.

As he walked down the road to Grandma's house, Bobby wondered why Grandma hadn't played a trick on him yet. Maybe she was saving it until the very last minute.

Bobby knocked on the big, wooden door.

"Hello, love." Grandma smiled
mischievously as she let him in.

"Come and have a look at Carrot the Goldfish! He's really settled in to his new home!"

"But Grandma," Bobby burst out. "It isn't a real goldfish! You see, it was my April Fool Trick. It's just a bit of carrot peel really!"

"Nonsense!" said Grandma. "Of course it's a real goldfish!"

"It isn't," Bobby insisted. "It was a joke! I never thought it'd fool you for so long!"

"Bobby, what are you talking about?" Grandma pretended to be puzzled. "It's a real goldfish. Come and see for yourself."

Bobby followed her into the lounge
and looked. Sure enough, there was
Carrot the Goldfish, swimming
energetically around his bowl.
Bobby's mouth dropped open in total
amazement.

36

"It's a goldfish!" he exclaimed.

"Well of course it's a goldfish," said Grandma. "What else would it be?"

Bobby was so surprised that he couldn't think of anything to say.

Suddenly Grandma burst out laughing. She laughed so much that her eyes watered.

"April Fool!" she cried triumphantly. "As soon as I realised you'd given me a bit of carrot peel, I thought of a brilliant trick to play on you. I went and replaced it with a real goldfish!"

"Grandma!" Bobby laughed. "You knew all along!"

"Yes," Grandma grinned. "And I've won the competition again this year for the best April Fool trick!"

Bobby gave her a big hug. "It was a brilliant trick," he agreed. "But mine was also good, wasn't it?"

"Oh yes," said Grandma. "In fact, it would probably have fooled me if I hadn't just got my new glasses yesterday." Bobby hadn't noticed the new glasses. They looked exactly the same as the old ones.

He didn't mind Grandma winning the competition again. He was too excited about the real goldfish, which was the prettiest little fish he'd ever seen.

"Can I come and visit him often?" Bobby asked.

"Of course," said Grandma. "He wouldn't be here if it wasn't for you!"